KING FLASHYPANTS

AND THE SNOWBALL OF DOOM

WRITTEN AND DRAWN BY **ANDY RILEY**

With thanks to Polly Faber,
Emma Goldhawk, Samuel Perrett,
Anne McNeil, Gordon Wise,
Hilary Murray Hill, Jennifer Stephenson,
Emily Thomas and Niall Harman

Dedicated to Eddie, Bill and Polly

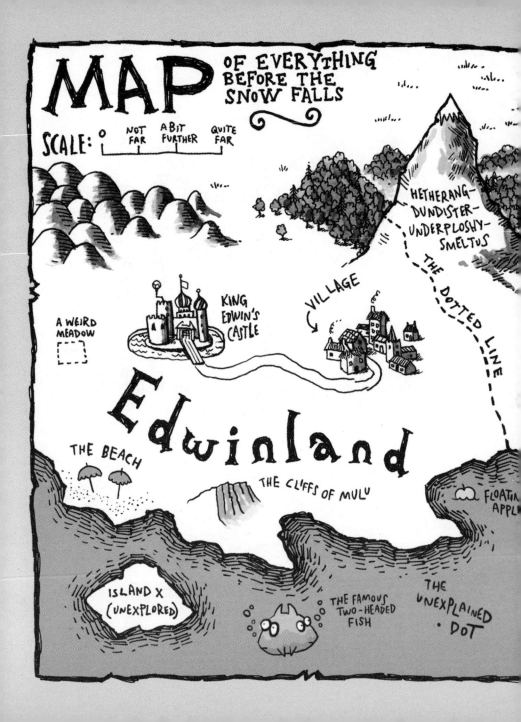

Chapters, Coming Right At You!

Summery Summer

It was hot in Edwinland. Really hot.

It was so hot that when people bought an ice cream from the van, it turned runny in two seconds and they had to pour it into their mouths like custard. It was so hot that you could fry eggs on the heads of bald men.

Lots of the children were doing just that. It was so hot that almost all the snow was gone from the tallest mountain in the land, **Hetherang-Dundister-Underploshy-Smeltus**. Only a teensy bit of white was left, just at the very top.

It was so hot that a rabbit running across a field suddenly melted, making a strange puddle with two ears sticking out. Half of Edwinland came to look. No one had seen anything like it.

So, all in all, things were on the warm side. Everybody in Edwinland had gone to have fun on the beach, and nobody was having more fun than King Edwin Flashypants himself. He was nine years old, which helped. Nine-year-olds are built for having fun. They are fun machines.

Edwin put a huge clump of seaweed on his head. He ran to Minister Jill, the clever grown-up who helped him with the difficult parts of being a king.

"Hello, Edwin," said Minister Jill.

"I'm not Edwin! I'm the seaweed monster who ate King Edwin! **GRAAAAHH!**"

"Hands out please, mister monster," she said, and she slapped half a bottle of sunblock on his arms.

"Look out Your Majesty, here comes the beach towel monster!" said Megan the Jester, who was very big and funny, and also King Edwin's best friend.

"Epic monster fight!" said Edwin, and they had a mighty battle, but in slow motion, because slow motion fights are the best fights.

" **GRAAAAHH!**, because

that's the noise seaweed monsters make!"

said the King.

"**Omm-Omm-Zubb** because

that's the noise beach towel monsters make!"

said the Jester,

who had

no idea

what noise

they really

did make, but

nobody there

could say she

was wrong.

Which she was, because they actually say

Chob-Chob-Flubb.

Edwin and Megan battled until they tripped over a sandcastle and fell flat on their backs. They laughed their heads off.

"Who thinks Edwin is the best king in the world?" shouted Megan.

WE DO!

said absolutely everyone.

And as they all laughed and danced in the sunshine, Edwin suddenly felt a little bit sad, and a little bit scared. But he didn't tell anyone why. He just kept smiling.

"Just going back to the castle for a nap," said Edwin.

"Righty ho," said Megan, who played a short song on her lute called *I'm About To Fall Asleep In a Deckchair*, then fell asleep in a deckchair.

"Don't forget to wash your feet, or you'll get sand on your duvet," said Minister Jill.

"I'll totally remember!" said Edwin.

A bit later, Edwin lay down in his big bedroom in his big castle. He burped into a big jar, then screwed the lid tight so it couldn't get out. He kept all his burps in the burp jar. Jill said it was a silly thing to do, but Edwin was sure he'd need those burps again some day.

Edwin was all alone, but it didn't feel like it.
For a few weeks now, Edwin had been hearing
a little voice inside his head. He called the voice
Wendy Worry.

They say you're the best king in the world, said Wendy to Edwin, *but they're as wrong as a hairy mirror.*

Can't you leave me alone for a bit? thought Edwin.

It's not like you're a proper king, from a proper royal family, said Wendy. *Maybe that's why you keep getting things wrong. Like those feet. Didn't wash them, did you?*

Edwin looked down at his sandy feet. *It's true, I didn't,* he thought. *I hoped you wouldn't notice.*

Okay, said Wendy, *you've seen off a few baddies like Emperor*

Nurbison and the Boo-Hoo Witches. But you've been lucky. Luck has to run out some time. Tell you what, let's have another think about exactly how you got to be a king in the first place . . .

Let's not, thought Edwin. *Let's think about fun and cool things, like a balloon doggie. Or haunted yoghurt. Or a stegosaurus on roller skates. Or a bar of soap made from cake, so you can eat and wash at the same time.*

Jill told you how it all happened, said Wendy. *Once upon a—*

But before Wendy Worry could tell him the rest of the story, Edwin sat up and stared out of the window.

Snow was falling. Not wet melty snow, or tiny light snow, but big fat lumpy snow. Real snow. **Snow** snow.

Right in the middle of summer.

Like, Really Chilly, Yeah?

"What people don't get about being evil is how much work goes into it," said a man with a tall black crown. "You can't just be wicked and cruel now and then, when the mood takes you. It's a lifetime's work. Oh, the stress."

The man with the crown was Emperor

Nurbison, and nobody worked harder at being
evil than he did. He lived in a tall scary castle
which he filled with deadly traps. If he didn't
like you, he pulled a lever and you fell into a
tank full of sharks. If he didn't like one of the

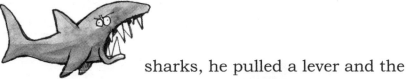

sharks, he pulled a lever and the

shark fell into a tank full of piranha

fish. If one of the piranhas just looked at him

funny, he pulled a lever and it fell into a

tank full of scorpions. If a

scorpion rolled its eyes,

Nurbison would have

pulled another lever,

but all these tanks cost

a lot of money to make, so he

would just whack the scorpion

with a big spoon.

"And no matter how evil I get, it's

never enough," sighed the emperor.

"Would you like to, you know, kind of punish me for, like, no reason?" said Globulus, the emperor's assistant, who was the exact size and shape of a beach ball.

"Well, that usually makes me feel better," said the emperor. "But while I'm being nasty to you, I'm not being nasty to King Edwin Flashypants. Or my peasants. See what I mean? I wish I could make a million jack-in-the-boxes, but inside each one, instead of a springy clown, there's a springy fist. I'd send one to every house in the world, to punch every face on earth, all at the same time. Ooh, hang on."

The emperor pulled out a leather notebook with "Future Evil Plans" written on the front in gold. Inside, he wrote:

One million springy fists (CHECK POSTAGE RATES)

Then he added a little sticker of a bear in dungarees, because he liked stickers of bears and he just didn't know why.

"Globulus, bring me the great big speaking tube."

Globulus held a metal pipe to the emperor's mouth. The pipe was linked up to a tower of

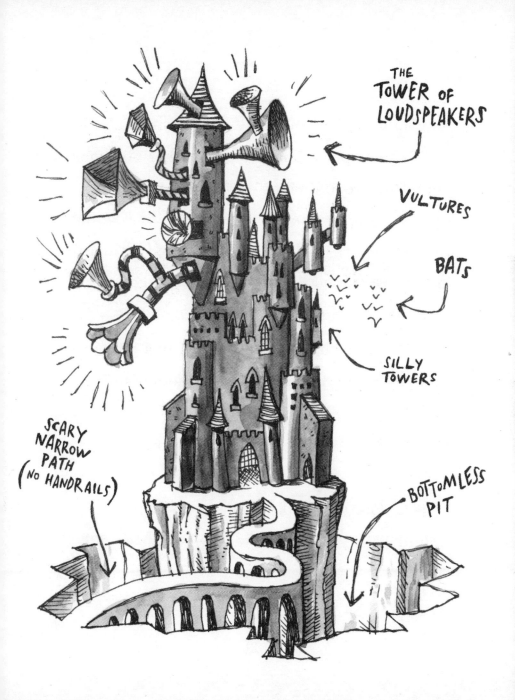

THE
TOWER OF
LOUDSPEAKERS

VULTURES

BATS

SILLY
TOWERS

SCARY
NARROW
PATH
(NO HANDRAILS)

BOTTOMLESS
PIT

loudspeakers on top of the castle. This was the emperor's favourite way of speaking to his poor subjects all over the land of Nurbisonia.

"Peasants! Hear me!" bellowed the Emperor. "I, the mighty Nurbison, say this: you no longer have to move piles of mud from one place to another, for no reason, twenty-four hours a day."

The Emperor paused for a few seconds.

"Because now you have to do it *twenty-seven hours a day*! And anyone who says there's only twenty-four hours in a day will have to do it *fifty-nine hours a day*.

FOO HOO HOO HOO!"

Foo Hoo Hoo Hoo was Emperor Nurbison's

special evil laugh. Often, he would write it in felt tip pen on Globulus's face when he was asleep, then not tell Globulus until lunchtime.

"Globulus, toddle outside and check on the P.M.L.," said Nurbison.

'P.M.L.' was short for 'Peasant Misery Level'. Globulus ran out of the castle on his tiny legs.

Five minutes later, he scampered back inside.

"P.M.L. is, you know, pretty high. Not just cos of the new mud rules, right, but also cos it's just gone, like, really chilly, yeah? Like a really amazingly super-cold sort of winter. Kind of thing."

The emperor threw open his creakiest wooden door and stepped outside. Snow whirled about and stuck in his incredibly handsome beard.

"I must be warm," said Nurbison, "warmer than anyone, because I'm the emperor! Globulus, make me a roaring fire. No, wait. It's not enough for me to be warm. Everybody else has to be as cold as a shaved puffin."

The emperor spotted a few peasants gathering sticks. *They might build themselves a fire,* he thought. *That won't do **at all.***

Nurbison had an army called the Sinister Soldiers. He sent them out to the mud fields to seize every last branch, stick and twig from the peasants. All the wood was loaded on to a big cart.

"Sinister soldiers!" said the emperor. "For

serving me well, you may build your own warm fire with this wood. Just kidding. It's all for me. Bye!" And he ran into his evil castle, pushing the cart with a Foo Hoo Hoo Hoo.

Soon the emperor sat by his largest fireplace, warming his toes and reading his favourite comic.

"I feel much happier now, Globulus,"
said Nurbison. "I've not been this mean to the
peasants in ages. Just think of them out there!
Shivering in their filthy rags! Hmm, I'm hungry.
Tell the kitchen to bring me a fried pig's nose
sandwich. With a bit of lettuce because I'm
trying to be healthy."

"Umm, well . . ." said Globulus. "Might be kind of a bit of a problem with that, your amazingness. All the cooks, they've sort of, run away, type of thing, cos it was too cold to stay here," said Globulus.

"Then send the sinister soldiers to catch them!" said Nurbison. "Durrr, as I believe the young emperors are saying."

"Yeah, but the soldiers have kind of totally run away as well."

"What!?" spat the emperor. "Then send my peasants, my loyal peasants, to catch the soldiers! Unless . . . Globulus, have they all run away too?"

Globulus nodded. He didn't have much of a neck to nod with, so he made his nod by rolling forwards and backwards.

"Scrunge!" shouted Emperor Nurbison. Because all this was happening in the olden days, their rude words were different to the ones you hear now.

He smashed the creaky door open. There was nobody outside – but there were plenty of footprints in the snow.

All of them heading west.

To Edwinland.

Proper Cosy

The people of Edwinland ran from the beach to Edwin's castle, going **"OOH"** and **"AHH"**, and **"BRRRRR"**, and **"AARGH WE'RE STILL IN OUR SWIMMING COSTUMES"**, because they were still in their swimming costumes.

Everyone dashed inside, wrapped
themselves in warm blankets, and huddled
around the biggest fireplace in the castle.

"Why has winter come in the middle of
summer?" said King Edwin.

Baxter, the castle's librarian and scientist, had already written down a few ideas. He read them out.

1. Unusual weather patterns

2. The world has been shut inside a giant space fridge

3. In a far-off desert kingdom, a child rubbed a lamp, and a genie came out and granted the child three wishes, and the child's first wish was for a winter so cold that

her bum shattered and fell to bits, and the genie said, are you sure? And the child said yes, that's what I want.

All three reasons sounded just as likely as each other.

"Why the mega-winter came isn't the important thing," said Minister Jill. "The question is, what do we do now it's here?"

Normally the right answer would be 'go and play in the snow', but it was so cold outside that Jill was worried their fingers might snap off like cheese straws.

"I know," said King Edwin. "We should get proper cosy!"

So that's just what they all did. They fed the fireplace with big crackling logs. They toasted marshmallows by the hundred. They even toasted toast, because when you toast toast that's already been toasted, you get toasted toast, and that's just the toastiest. The castle was so bright and snuggly and full of laughter that it almost drowned out the voice of Wendy Worry in Edwin's head.

"What would be the absolute best," said King Edwin, "would be if Megan the Jester sang us a song all about winter and snow and cosiness! Megan?"

Edwin looked around the throne room.

There were hundreds of people, but none of them were Megan. He thought she'd come in with everyone else. But had she really?

Well I've not seen her, said Wendy Worry. *Ooh, lovely! Something new to worry about!*

"Oh my goodness!" said Jill. "She must still be asleep in a deck chair! In her swimming costume! In the coldest winter for a hundred years!"

"There's not a moment to lose!" said King Edwin. Then he felt silly, because saying 'there's not a moment to lose' wastes about one and a half moments.

"Everybody stay here and keep warm," he said. "I'll ride out on my trusty horse to rescue her. Colin? We have a jester to save!"

King Edwin's faithful horse Colin galloped into the throne room.

"Neigh," said Colin.

Colin was brave, and he was loyal, and because he was a present bought for Edwin when Edwin was five, he was about as big as a medium-sized dog.

Soon the boy and his horse were galloping out of the castle. Edwin was in the warmest coat Jill could find, and he carried a thick furry rug to wrap Megan in when they found her. As Colin's little hooves thundered over the thickening snow, Edwin heard a shout from the castle: "Three cheers for King Edwin, the best king in the world!"

There they go again, said Wendy Worry, with that best-king-in-the-world stuff. But it's not true, is it Edwin? Is it? Is it? Is it? Look at me, Edwin! Is it?

A gasp-ulp came out of Edwin's mouth. Gasp-ulps are part gasp and part gulp. Edwin could *see* Wendy now.

She wasn't just a voice in his head any more – she was a full-on imaginary friend. Well, maybe 'friend' wasn't the right word, but there she was – a girl about Edwin's age, running alongside Colin.

You'll never find Megan in time, said Wendy. *She'll be frozen hard like a puddle of penguin pee.*

Edwin spurred Colin to run faster. But Wendy Worry kept up easily, as if she were taking a stroll in the park.

You can't outrun me, said Wendy. *Because
you're imagining me. You're such a stupid stupid
stupid stupid stupid stupid stupid stupid stupid*

stupid stupid stupid stupid stupid face. Anyway – what was it we were talking about, just before the snow came? Oh, I remember. How you got to be king in the first place.

Oh dear! thought Edwin, *I can't help it. I'm having a flashback. Here goes – wibble wobble wibble wobble wibble wobble . . .*

Chapter ZERO

The Flashback

Edwin had lost all the balls from his pool table, so he was playing pool with other round things, like gobstoppers and scotch eggs.

This bit wasn't happening while Edwin rode Colin the horse in the blizzard. This was happening in Edwin's castle, three weeks before

the snow fell, even before Chapter One. So this
is Chapter Zero. Of course, Edwin didn't know
what chapter he was in, as he potted a scotch
egg and made a shower of orange breadcrumbs.
Jill leaned over to sweep the table clean.

"Jill?" said King Edwin Flashypants. "I've been wondering. How did I get to become king? I meant to ask you three years ago when I was six, but then Megan ran in saying she'd just invented the fried chicken milkshake, so I had to go and try some, and ever since then I keep forgetting to ask. It can't be all that normal to be a king, can it? I mean, most people aren't kings."

Edwin was a clever boy who was very good at noticing things like that.

"Well . . . you're old enough to know the whole story," said Jill, in the voice grown-ups use when they're about to say something quite serious.

Edwin stopped playing pool to listen carefully, but he kept a scotch egg in his hand in case he got hungry.

"Long ago, before you were born, when I worked in the castle library, there was a good wise queen who ruled this land. Queen Millie. But one day, Queen Millie died of a large build-up of oldness. And she had no children to take the throne."

DUCHESS ROTHERA

"So whmm hummumm?" said Edwin, which is how you say "so what happened?" when you've got a mouthful of scotch egg.

"Queen Millie had two bad cousins," said Jill. "Baron Tostig and Duchess Rothera. They raised armies and fought each other for that crown you're wearing right now."

"Oh, a war! War is bad," said Edwin. "I know that. I learned it in a lesson about bad things. It's even worse

BARON TOSTIG

than some of the other bad things, like flat lemonade."

"This was a really rotten war, full of shouting and hitting," said Jill. "People were too scared to leave their houses to buy food. They couldn't even pop out for chocolate."

Wow! It must have been the worst war ever, thought Edwin.

"Then you arrived, Edwin. An orphan baby. The only survivor of a shipwreck, washed up on the beach.

I was the one who found you, and when I fed you and washed you, I saw the birthmark on your left foot."

"What, this one?" said Edwin, kicking off his shoe and putting his foot up on a chair. There was a brown birthmark, a bit like a triangle, but more lumpy.

Because it was the olden days and phones hadn't been invented yet, neither Minister Jill nor King Edwin knew that one day people like you would see a picture of the birthmark and say: 'hey, that looks a lot like the poo emoji.'

"And the moment I saw it, I knew just what it meant," said Minister Jill. "There was an old book of laws in the library which said, if the king or queen dies and has no child, then whoever has this birthmark shall rule. Next to a picture of a brown mark just like yours.

"So I showed the book to everyone, and everyone said 'this baby is the true king!' The armies threw down their hitty things and their jabby things. They tied Baron Tostig and Duchess Rothera to a goat, then frightened the goat, and we haven't seen them again.

"And you've been a wonderful king ever

since. Hooray for you! Now brush your teeth,

because you just ate five scotch eggs."

Later, when Jill was gone,
Edwin looked at his crown
in the mirror.

So I'm not quite a proper king, from a proper royal family, thought Edwin.

That's right, said a voice. *You're only the king because of a silly rule and a picture in a dusty old book.*

"Who's that?" said Edwin, out loud.

Just a voice in your head, said the voice. *We'll have lots of little chats from now on, you and me. Especially when you're worried.*

And that's how, three weeks before the snow fell, Wendy Worry came into Edwin's life.

4.
Find the Jester!

*So **that's** how you found out you aren't a proper king!* said Wendy Worry, as Edwin rode Colin through the whirling snow.

Not talking to you! Can't even see you! thought Edwin, shutting his eyes and covering his ears. *La la la la la. Oh, wait, I can't feel Colin under me.*

He must have stopped, and now I'm flying

through the air. Did he see something that scared

him? Or did he take a five-minute hay break?

Maybe I should open my eyes to find out. Yep,

that would be a good idea.

But before he could open his eyes, Edwin went **THONK**, head first, into something very hard.

He sat up, and looked up – into the shining blue eyes of a giant made of ice, with an ice face, and ice armpits, and ice teeth, and ice gums, and ice toes, and ice knees, and ice nostrils, and ice ears, and ice cheeks, and ice elbows, and ice knuckles, and ice shins, and ice kidneys, and ice fingernails, and ice eyelashes, and ice shoulders, so really there was no doubt about just how icy the thing was.

Which is why it also had ice arms, and ice thumbs, and ice eyebrows, and ice flanks, and

ice ankles, and ice heels, and ice knees, and ice biceps, and ice legbones, and ice calves, and ice nose hairs, and ice collarbones, and ice hips, and ice thighs, and ice lungs, and ice dimples.

And we haven't even talked about its ice lips. And ice abs, and ice pecs, and ice wrists, and ice ribs, and look – it was icy, okay? That's what it was. Very icy.

"AAAAAARRGGHH!" said Edwin. Then he remembered he must always be polite to people, even terrifying looming ice giants.

"AAAAAARRGGHH and good day to you!" said Edwin.

The ice giant turned and ran into the blizzard.

"What, who, when, and all the other question words!" said Edwin, gasp-ulping. He'd never seen a person made of ice before.

Ice monsters in Edwinland! said Wendy. *More and more for you to worry about. Oh, what a day! Oh, what a lovely day!"*

On the beach, Megan woke up.

"Wonder if I'm getting a tan?" she said, stretching.

She looked at her hand. It was much whiter than before.

"Bit weird," said Megan. "Oh, silly me! It's just five centimetres of snow, all over me."

She lay back in the deck chair. Ten seconds later, she jumped right out of it.

"Five centimetres of snow all over me! I'm freezing! And I'm just in my swimsuit! Ooh! Aah! Ooh!"

She tried to wrap herself in a towel, but the towel was frozen so hard that it snapped in two.

Just as Megan was trying to start a fire by rubbing two icicles together, King Edwin burst out of a snowdrift, riding Colin.

"You're totally saved, Megan!" said the King, and he wrapped her in the big rug.

"Hooray!" said the jester. "Hooray with a tasty side of Yippee!"

"Now let's get you home to the castle," said Edwin. "I thought about this before I set off. It'll

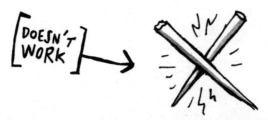

be easy to find our way home. We just follow Colin's hoof prints," said Edwin.

"Neigh," said Colin.

This was horse language for 'but, good friends, the marks of my powerful hooves have disappeared in the falling snow.'

It was true – they were gone. Edwin couldn't see the road, or his castle, or even the mountain of Hetherang-Dundister-Underploshy-Smeltus, and normally you could see that from anywhere.

"Well, that's the way home, I think, definitely, probably!" said Edwin, pointing into the raging blizzard.

Colin tried to gallop, but now the snow was
too thick for his little horse legs.

"Still got your bucket and spade, Megan?"
said Edwin.

Megan pulled them out from under her jester's hat.

"Great!" said Edwin. "If we can't ride home, we can dig our way home."

King Edwin and Megan the Jester dug, and dug, and dug, cutting a trench through the deepening snow. The wind got colder and colder. It blew through Edwin and played his leg bones like flutes.

"Think hot thoughts!" said Edwin. "That'll help. Hot, hot, hot, hot, hot! Wow, I'm so boiling hot!"

"Hot, hot, hot-t-t-t-t," said Megan, her teeth chattering like those wind-up ones from gift shops. "Are you really *really* sure this is the right way, Edwin?"

"T- T- T- totally!" he said, hurling another bucketload of snow over his shoulder.

You SO don't know that, said Wendy Worry, turning cartwheels for fun. *You're lost, like a chicken on the moon.*

Megan was pointing.

"Wh-wh- what are those?" she said.

Through the whirling blizzard, Edwin could just make out the ice giant watching them from behind a snowdrift. And it wasn't alone. Other blue eyes shone beside it.

"Oh, don't worry about those icy creatures!" said Edwin, brightly. "I *definitely* didn't make them angry by head-butting one of them on the way here. **In no way did I do that.** And even if I did, it hardly matters because we're totally, maybe, nearly at the castle!"

Edwin dug through a very big snowdrift –

And nearly fell over a cliff.

"Ah, right," said Edwin. "I know what's happened here. We're at the Cliffs of Mulu."

"Isn't it the Cliffs of Mulu which have a two hundred metre drop, straight down to a patch of Sawtooth Greenhorrors, the world's deadliest stinging nettles?" said Megan.

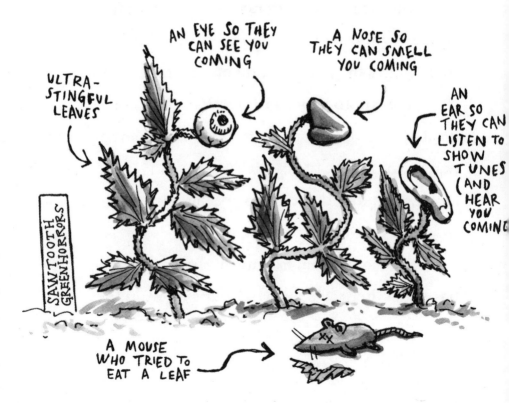

AN EYE SO THEY CAN SEE YOU COMING

A NOSE SO THEY CAN SMELL YOU COMING

ULTRA-STINGFUL LEAVES

AN EAR SO THEY CAN LISTEN TO SHOW TUNES (AND HEAR YOU COMING

SAWTOOTH GREENHORRORS

A MOUSE WHO TRIED TO EAT A LEAF

"Yep, those cliffs," said Edwin. "So maybe we need a tiny change of direction. Let's try digging . . . **that** way."

Edwin pointed.

"Totally the other way to where we were just going?" said Megan.

"Umm . . . yes!" said Edwin.

After another hour of frantic bucket and spade work, Edwin and Megan saw Edwin's castle looming before them. Not looming in a scary way like the icy giant, but in a friendly way.

"I've never seen such nice looming," said Megan.

At the castle gates, there were three ways
to ask to get in: a huge horn, a big doorknocker,
and a massive doorbell with a red button a
metre wide. As it was a bit of an emergency,
Edwin, Megan and Colin used all three at once.

BANG-BANG-DING-DONG-PAAARRRRPPP!

The drawbridge came down, and there was Minister Jill.

"Two did leave – but three return!" said Edwin, who had been waiting to say that for hours, because it sounded cool.

"Looks more like seven hundred and seventy six to me," said Jill.

"No, I reckon it's three," said Edwin.

"I've just counted," said Jill. "I'm very sure it's seven hundred and seventy six."

Edwin turned round. Behind him was a field full of sad-looking peasants, shivering and huddling together.

"King Edwin?" said a peasant. "We're from Nurbisonia. C- C- can we come into your castle, j-j-just for a bit? We need to keep warm and the Emperor won't even let us burn one piece of straw."

"You've come to the right place," said King Edwin. "We've got a fire, hot chocolate, hot water bottles, and biscuits as big as frisbees, straight from the oven. Come in!"

The peasants and the soldiers hurried into Edwin's castle. Every one of them stopped to thank the young king on the way in.

See, Wendy? thought Edwin. *I did save Megan. And now everybody's safe and warm,* and we've just made some new friends.

And, said Wendy, *Emperor Nurbison's going to be a teeny tiny bit angry when he works out where his peasants are.*

La la la la la! thought Edwin, loudly. *Can't hear you,* **la la la la, la la la, la la, la la la la la la la oh hang on you're right.**

Hear Me Now

By the next morning, it had stopped snowing. The sun rose into a clear blue sky.

Edwin boinged to the top of his highest tower in one of the castle's many boingers.

He looked all around. The world was smothered in a crisp blanket of snow. The mountain of Hetherang-Dundister-Underploshy-Smeltus gleamed white from top to bottom. All was calm. All was quiet.

Except for the screaming, shouting man just outside the castle.

Yes, the screaming, shouting man definitely brought the noise levels up a bit.

"Peasants!" yelled Emperor Nurbison. "MY peasants! I know you're in there! Hiding in the castle of my enemy, King Edwin Flashypants!"

"Hi, Emperor Nurbison," said Edwin, waving.

Everyone in the castle leaned out of the windows.

"Leaving the mighty Empire of Nurbisonia is a massive crime," said the emperor. "Perhaps the crimey-est of all the crimes. What's the punishment for that one, Globulus?"

"Errrr – let's see –" said Globulus. "Yeah, I know. Eating live worm sandwiches for like a whole a year. But with no ketchup and no butter. And no bread. So, you know, it's just eating a great big load of live worms, more or less."

"Mmm, yummy live worms," said Nurbison. "But, ungrateful peasants, if you all come back right away, I will only make you eat them for half a year. Because I love you all."

The emperor did his 'nice' face. He could only hold it for a few seconds. It was a big strain.

'NICE'
FACE

"You don't love us," somebody shouted. "You never even learned our names."

"Not true! I've got names for just about all of you," said the emperor.

He pointed at one peasant.

"You're 'Lazy Peasant'," he said.

He pointed at a second peasant.

"You're 'Smelly Peasant'."

He pointed at a third.

"You're 'Some Other Peasant'. See? Lots of names!"

"Edwin doesn't even call them peasants at all," said Megan the Jester.

"Yeah, I stopped using that word," said

Edwin. "Now I say, 'valued members of the empowered citizen client group'."

King Edwin didn't know what any of those words meant, but he'd read them in Jill's 'Minister Monthly' magazine when she'd left a copy lying open on the back of a goat, and they sounded about right. Nicer than 'peasants', anyway.

"Scrunge! Just give them back, Edwin!" said the emperor. "Actually, Globulus, I need an even ruder word than scrunge to really get my point across."

"Umm, errr, there isn't one, your fantasticness," said Globulus.

"WELL, THINK ONE UP!"

Globulus had a think, then whispered in Nurbison's ear. Nurbison nodded.

"Edwin, give me back my peasants,"
said the emperor, "or you are a big, stinky
CLOFFBODGE."

Everyone was amazed by this new word.
As olden days rudeness went, 'cloffbodge' was
completely off the scale. Grown-ups covered
their children's ears, and children covered their
dollies' ears.

Edwin said, "Open the drawbridge please,"
and down it clanked.

"Everyone's free to choose. If you want to
head back to Nurbisonia with the emperor –
there he is."

Everyone stayed just where they were.

"FINE!" said the emperor, in exactly that way people do when nothing is fine at all. "But every last one of you, hear me now. *Emperor Nurbison is not finished with you.*"

The emperor gave them a long, cold stare.

"The emperor is, like, you know, giving you a long cold stare," said Globulus.

"Just the sort of stare which works better

when it doesn't come with a commentary," said Nurbison.

"Oh, sorry," said Globulus.

And the emperor stomped away, but the snow was so deep that his boots just went 'flumff' not 'stomp', so Globulus had to do the sound effects with his mouth.

"Stomp! Stomp! Errr, kinda like, Stomp, sort of thing!" said Globulus, as they both dodged snowballs chucked by the valued members of the empowered citizen client group.

Emperor Nurbison and Globulus trudged back towards the emperor's castle. It was so cold that the emperor's eyes began to chatter. If it's cold enough, any bit of you can chatter, not just teeth, but other parts like your hair or your bum.

"G– G– Globulus. Warm me," said the emperor.

A white arctic fox ran past. Globulus scampered around until he caught it, plus another fourteen or fifteen. Then he stuffed all the foxes up the emperor's cloak. They were a bit wriggly and scratchy, but they kept the emperor cosy enough.

"I suppose these white creatures were living on the snowy bits of the mountain all this time," said the Emperor. "But now it's cold and icy everywhere, they can run where they like. Or they could! Until we caught them!"

The emperor shouted into his cloak.

"Foxes! You work for Emperor Nurbison now! **FOO HOO HOO HOO!**"

"What about, like, these other guys?"
said Globulus, "Have they been, like, living up
the mountain all this time too? Kind of thing?"

The emperor looked up – and into the face
of the ice giant with the bright blue eyes.

It had an ice face.

And ice teeth.

If you can't remember all the other icy parts
it had, you can always go back and check.

The giant and its odd-shaped ice friends
watched the emperor carefully.

"Whatever they are, they're pretty stupid-

looking things," said the emperor. "Strange and stupid and ugly. I don't think they understand anything we say."

"Unless we can," said the spiky giant, speaking perfect Human.

"Whoops," said Emperor Nurbison.

Meet the Ice Folk

"Alright, I might have called you stupid and ugly," said the emperor to the icy creatures, "but you shouldn't hurt me because I am SUCH a nice person. Aren't I, Globulus?"

"What? Oh, yeah," said Globulus. "He's a very lovely evil emperor. I mean, a very lovely emperor. Yeah. Totally."

"And I was just on my way to save baby animals at my baby animal sanctuary," said the emperor.

The giant and her friends looked at each other, then opened their mouths and tinkled loudly while their shoulders wobbled.

"Emperor?" said Globulus. "I think they're, you know, I think they're laughing."

"You're evil," said the spiky giant, "of that I am sure. It's the black cloak. And the black boots. That beard. That crown."

"Solid look," said an ice cube with legs.

"Very well! I admit it!" said the emperor. "I am the very evil Emperor Nurbison. I am harsh, and cruel, and I'll put bin juice into other peoples' milkshakes. But I can't harm you. Look: I have no army."

The emperor waved his arm in the general direction of a snowy field, where an army definitely wasn't.

"You know who I am," said Emperor Nurbison. "And now I wish to learn all about you. Who are you? Where are you from? What's your standard order from the chip shop? Can you play the trombone? How do you organise your shoes? Do you even have shoes? If a tree falls down in the forest and nobody's there, does it makes a sound? How many custard cream biscuits can you fit in your mouth at once? Can you tie a balloon, or do you need a grown-up to help?"

The icy creatures looked confused.

"All right, too many questions," said Emperor Nurbison. "Let's stick to the first two."

The spiky giant said, "I am Crystalface, the chief of all the ice folk. We come from the peak of the mountain."

She pointed to Hetherang-Dundister-Underploshy-Smeltus.

"That mountain," she said, "which we call Hetherang-Dundister-Underploshy-Smeltus."

"Like, wow," said Globulus. "We call it Hetherang-Dundister-Underploshy-Smeltus too."

"So we all call it Hetherang-Dundister-

Underploshy-Smeltus, then," said the ice cube, who was called Cube.

"Look," said the emperor. "If we all keep calling it that, this chat will take ages. Let's call it 'Hetherang' from now on to save a little time.

Yes? Good. It's Hetherang. Much better. Carry on."

"The last month was the worst we ever knew," said Chief Crystalface. "The heat! Only a tiny patch of snow was left at Hetherang's peak. My people can only live in frozen places. If the last snow melts, we melt with it."

The ice folk whimpered, in a tinkly sort of way.

"But yesterday – a miracle!" said Chief Crystalface. "More snow than anyone can remember. We can explore the world!"

Ah, thought Emperor Nurbison. *They love the cold, they're afraid of the warm. I wonder if an evil plan will pop into my head in the next few seconds? Ah! It did. I'm so clever, it's as if my mind has a mind.*

"It's been delightful to meet you," said the emperor. "Must get back to my castle now. Bye-bye! Oh, and good luck against King Edwin the Hot."

The emperor walked away, whistling.

"Emperor!" called Chief Crystalface. "Who is King Edwin the Hot?"

"Oh, you don't know about him?" said Emperor Nurbison, spinning round, slipping over in the snow, then standing up quickly like he hadn't slipped at all.

"King Edwin the Hot is a nine-year-old boy. He lives in that castle over there. And he loves hot things. Absolutely loves them, he does. Let me explain . . ."

The ice folk gathered round Emperor Nurbison as he told them lies about King Edwin. He told them about a boy who drank a mug of lava with his breakfast, who washed his hair in boiling shampoo, who had built a spaceship so he could take holidays on the surface of the sun.

"I think we have seen this boy," said Chief Crystalface.

"The one who kept saying hot, hot, hot, hot?" said one ice creature.

"And gave you a flying head butt?" said another.

A loud tinkly murmuring filled the air.

"You know why it was so scorching lately, don't you?" said Emperor Nurbison. "Because King Edwin the Hot invented a magic heat machine to boil the world. I heard it broke yesterday and that's why everything's cold now. But then I heard – oh dear, I can hardly say it, it's so upsetting."

The emperor wobbled his beard around as if he was about to cry.

"I heard he's building a new machine to boil the whole world. It'll melt every last bit of snow on this planet."

The Emperor pointed a shaking finger at

Edwin's castle. Its biggest chimney was smoking merrily.

"See the smoke from his factory! Edwin's machine will be ready soon. Oh, I may be evil, but there are worse people in the world even than I."

"How do we stop this boy monster?" the chief said.

"Together, that's how!" said Nurbison.

The ice folk took three steps back.

"What's the matter, Globulus?" said the emperor. "Are they afraid of me suddenly?"

"Umm, no," said Globulus. "One of the foxes in your cloak just, you know, did a fox poo."

There was a small smelly mound under Nurbison's cloak.

"Pretty sure it's a fox poo," said Globulus, "cos if you think about it, a fox poo must be the only poo a fox can do, eh? I mean, it's, you know, it's not going to do a dolphin poo. Only a

dolphin can do a dolphin poo. Only a gnu could do a gnu poo. That's, you know, how the whole pooing business works. Probably. Haven't given it a lot of thought until now."

"Globulus," said the emperor, "whatever sort of poo it is, just put it in your hat to get rid of later. Right, where was I? Oh yes. Together, that's how!"

The emperor climbed on to the shoulder of his new giant friend. Globulus sat on Cube.

"Chief Crystalface? Take us up the mountain!" said Nurbison.

King Edwin Flashypants and those horrible peasants have no idea what's coming, thought the emperor.

But they will soon.

They will soon.

Building the Thing

It was so cold at the peak of Hetherang that lightning bolts and rainbows would freeze in mid-air, then fall to the mountainside with a great **CLANG**. Emperor Nurbison gathered bits of frozen lightning to make a very sharp and glowing throne.

First the ice folk built a huge platform made of icicles, right across the mountain's thin peak. Then, on top of that, they began to build a gigantic globe of snow.

"It's, you know, going to be a totally massive snowball, kind of thing," said Globulus. "Even bigger than, like, King Edwin's castle."

"It has to be," said Emperor Nurbison. "My peasants dared to throw snowballs at me! Well, before night falls, I shall drop *my* snowball on *them*.

And then Edwin, the peasants, the castle and everyone in it, will all be squashed flat as marzipan! Foo hoo hoo hoo!"

"Yeah. Classic," said Globulus. "But, you know, marzipan can be any shape, can't it? Little flowers, or tiny model people, or—"

"Flat marzipan!" said the emperor.

"All right? Marzipan is always very very flat."

Globulus knew that marzipan isn't always flat, but it was best to let the emperor have that one. 'Letting him have that one' is an important skill to learn if you're ever going to be an evil emperor's assistant.

Cube shuffled past, carrying a mound of snow on his head.

"Dude," said Cube to Globulus.

"Dude," said Globulus. "Good work carrying all that snow on your head, yeah? If it is a head, cos I suppose when you're just a cube with legs, it's hard to know what's your head and what's your bum, kind of thing."

"Tell me about it," said Cube. "But I've been thinking – what if this 'King Edwin the Hot' guy just doesn't know much about us? If we just tell him who we are, what we're made of, then maybe he won't turn his world-boiling machine on. And we won't need to squish him."

Nurbison stomped toward Cube.

"Chief Crystalface!" the emperor said. "A traitor questions the snowball! How will you punish him? Me, I'd fire him from my biggest cannon straight down the castle toilets, but everyone's got their own style, haven't they."

"All are free to speak their minds here,"
said Chief Crystalface.

"What a charming local tradition!" said the
emperor. "Cube, dear friend, explain your idea
to me again, please."

"Well, the way I see it—" said Cube.

"No, not here," said the emperor. "Round
there, behind that huge pile of
icicles."

"Yeah, round there,
where nobody can
see," said Globulus.

So they went round the back of the icicles, and as soon as Cube repeated "well, the way I see it", the emperor kind-of-accidentally-but-not-really-accidentally pushed into Cube's head, or bum, or whatever it was.

And knocked him right off the mountain.

"WHOOPS!" said the emperor.

Cube tumbled through the air, then bounced down the mountainside until he fell through the clouds and out of sight.

"I think he was sort of becoming my friend, though," said Globulus.

"Oh, Globulus," said the Emperor. "You know I don't like you having friends."

"Yeah, umm, spotted that," said Globulus.

Down in Edwin's castle, Edwin had invented a machine. Not a world-boiling machine which would melt the ice folk, though. It was

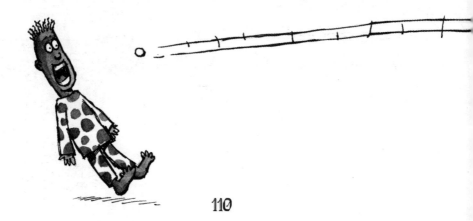

a machine which fired toasted marshmallows
into your mouth at thirty miles per hour. This
machine wouldn't hurt a fly, just so long as the
flies kept well clear.

All of Nurbison's peasants had got rid of the
rotting sacks he made them wear. The people
of Edwinland had given them snuggly pyjamas
with fun patterns on.

said Megan the Jester.

The emperor had never allowed his subjects nice things like 'pyjamas' and 'parties', never mind both at once. The new arrivals were so happy they could burst, and three of them actually did, so it was a good job Jill had a first aid kit.

King Edwin looked around. He saw people drinking hot chocolate, and cuddling hot water bottles, and having pillow fights. Wendy Worry was still there, watching him, but she kept quiet in the corner of the room.

All's well, thought Edwin. *The emperor might be angry but there's nothing he can do about it. Maybe I really **am** okay at being a king.*

*And I know I've thought before that nothing will ever go wrong ever ever ever again, and I've always been wrong. But maybe **this** time it's really true!*

There was a loud

as something crashed through the castle's big back door. Then another smash, and another. Something hard was moving at amazing speed.

A final SMASH, and the door of the throne room turned to flying splinters. Something skidded across the floor and came to a stop right in front of Edwin, Megan and Jill.

Something none of them had seen before.

Something icy.

Something alive.

The Expedition

"Wow, wow, and thrice wow!" said Megan the Jester.

'Thrice' was a word they had in the olden days which meant 'three times'. It was just one of many words people threw away in a big pile at the end of the olden days. Then those old words got recycled into modern words, like hench and peng.

"It's a pair of eyes in a frozen block!" said King Edwin. "Whatever it is, the poor thing is stuck in a lump of ice. Quick, let's melt it out."

Megan fetched two of the biggest hot water

bottles, and slapped Cube in the middle to make an icy sandwich. Melted water dribbled on to the floor.

"Eek!" said Cube, wriggling away.

"Oh no, it fell out. Hold it next to the roaring fire!" said King Edwin. Megan held Cube near the flames.

"No no no no no no!" said Cube, his little legs thrashing in the air.

"I don't think it's inside the cube," said

Minister Jill. "I think it *is* the cube. It's some sort of ice creature."

"Oh yeah!" said Edwin. "Like the ones I saw before. Sorry."

Edwin cracked open a window, scraped a big pile of snow from the sill, and plonked Cube in the middle of it.

"Phew! Thank you," said Cube.

Baxter ran in clutching a small book.

"I've found an Ice-Creature-To-Human dictionary, so I'll translate for everybody," said Baxter.

"How do I say *sorry for giving your friend a flying headbutt?*" said Edwin.

"Tinkle tinkle tinkle," said Baxter.

"It's okay, I can talk Human," said Cube.

Baxter studied the book for half a minute.

"He said . . . *it's okay, I can talk Human,*" said Baxter. Even though everyone knew what Baxter was doing was totally pointless, it made him feel useful, so nobody stopped him.

People gathered round Cube and asked questions like:

- How can you be a piece of ice *and* be alive at the same time?

- How do you keep your corners sharp?

- Which part of you is your head and which part is your bum or are they both the same?

And once Cube had answered them, he turned to King Edwin.

"So, you must be King Edwin the Hot."

"No one's ever called me that," said Edwin. "I'm King Edwin Flashypants."

"Well, it's what they call you up there," said Cube. "I'm one of the ice folk, from the top of

Hetherang-Dundister-Underploshy-Smeltus."

"There's folk?" said Megan. "At the top of Hetherang-Dundister-Underploshy-Smeltus?"

"Yes, on Hetherang-Dundister-Underploshy-Smeltus. But lately we've been calling it Hetherang, to save a bit of time."

"Excellent idea," said Minister Jill.

Cube told Edwin how the ice folk thought
he was making a big machine to boil the world.

"I wouldn't do that!" said King Edwin.
"Snow is the best!"

"Edwin doesn't want to destroy the ice
folk," said Jill. "When he meets new people, he
always remembers to not wipe them out."

"Yes, you've brought him up
very well," said
Megan.

Cube said, "I believe you. Or you'd be melting me into a puddle now. But it doesn't matter what I think, because up on the mountain they're making a giant snowball to squish this castle flat. And everyone in it!"

"Gasp-ulp!" said the people of Edwinland.

"That would totally ruin my pyjama party," said Megan.

"I said I didn't like the plan, and that's when he shoved me down the mountain," said Cube.

"Who shoved you?" said Minister Jill. "Wait, let me guess. Does he have a black crown?"

"And a black cloak," said Cube, "and black

boots, and a little beard, and nothing you could call a nose, and his name is—"

said King Edwin.

"You know him too?" said Cube. "Small world."

"All right," said Edwin, "so Emperor Nurbison told the ice folk I'm the worst thing in the universe, and he's got them making a giant snowball that'll crush us all. I'll just have to climb that mountain and stop it from happening."

Cube stepped forward.

"You'll need a guide," he said.

"And a jester!" said Megan.

Megan thought jesting was the most important job in the world, and she was absolutely right.

Everybody cheered. Cheering is great fun, and in Edwinland they did it at all the time, even when they had no idea just what they were cheering about.

"Me, Megan and Cube are going on an expedition," said King Edwin. "Jill, you keep everybody warm and safe in the castle, but look out for a three hundred metre snowball falling through the clouds. If you see that, that's a bad thing, worse than flat lemonade, and everybody should run outside. Cube, Megan – let's go!"

"Wait," said Minister Jill. "Shouldn't you and Megan put on something warm over your pyjamas?"

So they did.

"Okay," said King Edwin, "let's go!"

"Just a sec," said Minister Jill. "Maybe you should stuff your coats with hot water bottles. And how about some climbing ropes, a tent, things like that?"

So they gathered all that stuff together.

"Right!" said King Edwin. "Megan, Cube, let's – actually, maybe you should come too, Jill. You always think of all kinds of clever things that we don't."

So Jill pulled on her coat, and stuffed it with hot water bottles, then Baxter was put in charge of the castle, then Baxter tripped over his beard and bashed his nose, then Colin the horse was put in charge of the castle, then Edwin packed his jar of burps in case it came in handy, and then – finally – they were ready.

The drawbridge clanked down. King Edwin Flashypants, Minister Jill, Megan the Jester, and Cube the Cube, all stood ready to leave.

"Four friends to save the day!" said Megan.

Oh, there's five of us though, said a familiar voice.

Edwin slowly turned his head.

There was Wendy Worry. And she was doing the macarena.

I'm coming, of course! said Wendy. *I said your luck would run out some time,*

and today's the day! The tallest mountain ever,
a giant snowball, ice monsters . . . and Emperor
Nurbison. Maybe a proper king could handle all
those at once. But not a rubbish king like you, eh,
Edwin?

"I hate you and your stupid pigtails!" said
King Edwin.

"Who's that you're talking to?" said
Minister Jill.

"Absolutely nobody and nothing at all!" said
King Edwin.

I AM a proper king, thought Edwin. *I am, I*
am, I am!

"Minister Jill?" said Edwin. "Before we go,

can we run up to the library, and see the old book of laws? The bit about the birthmark and being the true king? I just need to see it for myself."

They dashed up to the castle library, and Jill heaved open the huge book.

"Let's see your birthmark then," said Jill. Edwin pulled off his overboot, his boot, his underboot, his oversock, his sock, his undersock and his under-undersock.

There was the brown birthmark.

"Now, let's look at page eight-nine-three," said Jill. "If the old queen or king dies without a son or a daughter, the one with this brown mark upon their skin shall have the – ah! Ummm – the crown."

Edwin stared at the page, then at his foot, then at the page. The picture looked just like his birthmark – only it wasn't brown like Jill said it would be. It was a sort of yellow colour.

FAINT
&
YELLOWY

Ooooooh, there's something very strange here, said Wendy Worry. *That picture's the wrong colour altogether. And just look at Jill. She got all nervous when she saw it. You and me, we can have a GREAT old worry about THIS.*

And off they all marched, across the crisp snow – the four of them, plus Wendy, who carried a big flag which said 'Edwin Is Such A Loser'.

"Nobody look at the large imaginary flag!" said Edwin.

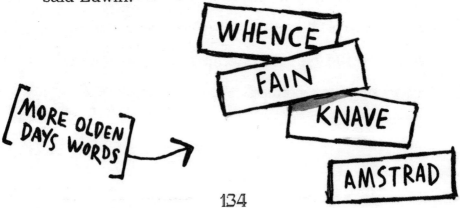

MORE OLDEN DAYS WORDS →

WHENCE

FAIN

KNAVE

AMSTRAD

To the Summit!

The mountain of Hetherang towered before them. It was so tall that if you got a thousand elephants and threw them all in a big pile, that pile still wouldn't be half as tall as the mountain, and you'd have a thousand quite angry elephants. It would be no use apologising and offering them free buns, because they would be busy writing angry letters to your mum. Also they would be kicking your face round to the back of your head.

As it got steeper, Edwin and his friends switched from walking to climbing with ropes and hooks. Being one of the ice folk, Cube knew all about climbing Hetherang, and was

always ready with useful advice like 'just try not to fall off, yeah?'

Up and up they went. And after they went up and up, they went up. Then up a bit more. Then up.

Yes, 'up' was really the only way to go.

"Hey, we're above the clouds!" said Megan, because they were above the clouds.

"Don't look down, Edwin," said Jill.

"Don't worry, I won't," said Edwin, looking down.

Big fluffy clouds danced around below them, and on top of the clouds, fluffy faces looked at him and waved.

People! Living in the clouds! thought King Edwin. *First ice folk, then cloud folk. I've found all kinds of new beings lately. When this adventure is over, I must remember to have an adventure with the cloud people.*

Edwin got out a leather notebook. On the front, gold lettering said 'Adventures I Haven't Had Yet But Would Like To.' Inside was a list:

-An Adventure with Aliens
  -An Undersea Adventure (make sure
    to invent submarines first, or get
    very good at holding breath)
  -A Cowboy Adventure where I get
    to hang on the bottom of a
    stagecoach and a baddie falls
    backwards into a horse trough
  -An Adventure in a Big City where
    I end up on a parade float and
    everyone's cheering
  -An Adventure Where I Get To
    Feed Baby Lambs
  -An Adventure With Talking Trees
    that are really wise because
    talking trees always are

At the bottom, Edwin wrote 'An adventure with the cloud people.'

Stop enjoying yourself, said Wendy Worry. *That's no way to carry on.*

Climbing was easy for Wendy – she just walked up the side of the mountain like gravity didn't matter.

Imaginary people are so annoying sometimes.

"Come on Edwin," said Jill. "We can't stop for long. The water bottles in our coats won't stay hot forever."

"Look! You can see our castle from here," said Edwin. "And smoke from the chimney. At

least everybody there
is toasty warm."

"Oh yeah,"
said Cube. "That
smoke's a bit of
a problem. The
ice folk reckon it's
from your factory where
you're building the machine
to boil the world."

"Cube?" said Jill. "Do you think it would've been good for us to know a bit earlier, when we were all down there, and we could have put the fireplace out for a while?"

Cube thought for a few seconds, then said, "Ummmmm . . . yeah. Sorry."

Oh dear oh dear oh dear! said Wendy. *The smoke makes the ice people even more scared, and soon they'll push the giant snowball down the mountain, and Colin and Baxter and everyone will be squished as flat as omelettes! Try not to imagine them as omelettes.*

Well I just did, because you said it!
said Edwin. *Stop saying I shouldn't think of something, because that makes me think of that thing, and you know it does.*

Ooh! Tricky bit of climbing coming up, said Wendy. *Try not to think about falling off because then you really **might** fall. DO NOT think about falling. Or plummeting. Or dropping. Or plunging . . .*

Edwin was trying so hard to not listen to Wendy that he missed a handhold. Edwin slipped. And fell.

WHOOSH! Edwin dropped straight past Jill, Megan and Cube.

"Just need to . . . reach into my pack . . . for the jar of burps . . ." said Edwin, reaching into his pack for the jar of burps.

He unscrewed the lid and released two hundred and seven burps from the jar. Almost a month's worth. The awesome power of the burps rocketed him back up the cliff and he grabbed on to the ice again.

"Hooray!" said Megan.

"And a tiny bit disgusting," said Minister Jill.

"Nearly at the top now," said Cube.

*That was **such** a scary fall,* said Wendy. *Look, Edwin, you're shaking! Shaky, shaky, shake, and not just from the cold.*

"Before we go up the last bit, let's rest a moment," said Jill. She opened a plop tent, which get their name because when you unzip them they plop into the right shape with a plop sound. Edwin, Megan and Jill crawled inside. Cube stayed outside – to keep watch, he said – but really because he was too embarrassed to look Jill in the eye after the whole smoke-from-the-fireplace business.

"I'm eeeever so tired from climbing," said Megan. "But we're about to face the evil emperor and that's very important, so I won't fall asleep like I did on the beach." Then she fell asleep.

Jill said, "how are you feeling, Edwin? You look a bit – well, a bit worried."

"I'm *very* worried," said Edwin. "Jill, do you ever get a voice inside your head saying how rubbish you are? And sometimes you see it too, like an imaginary friend?"

"Now and again," said Minister Jill. "He's

called Baron Von Fretty.
He's a purple blob with
a top hat and a big curly
moustache, and he says
things like *Jill, you're a
walking disaster!* But I
order him to go away with
my best telling-off voice, and that gets rid of him
for a while. Why do you ask, Edwin? Do you
have an imaginary not-a-friend too?"

"Never, no, never had one, don't know why I
started talking about it really," said Edwin. But
he didn't even need to look at Jill to know she
didn't believe him.

"Jill," said Edwin. "That picture in the book. It wasn't brown like the mark on my foot. It was yellow."

"Oh, that's not important, it's not even a thing, and that's all there is to it," said Jill.

"Shall we tell each other the truth, Jill?" said King Edwin. "I'll go first. I **do** have an imaginary not-a-friend, and her name is Wendy Worry."

Now it was Jill's turn. She tried to speak thrice before she could get any words out.

"The picture in the book, the one that looks like your birthmark," said Jill. "It's not as old as I said it was. *I* made the mark in the book."

Edwin's mouth fell open. Jill pushed his chin back up again in case his tongue froze like a rocket lolly.

"Everyone was fighting and people were getting hurt!" said Jill. "I had to do something.

So when I found you, a beautiful little baby with a funny little brown bit on your foot, I had an idea. I drew a picture of your brown mark on a blank page in an old book, and invented a rule to go with it, then I showed it to everyone. I sort of . . . made the whole thing up."

Jill looked like she was about to cry.

"But that was nearly nine years ago, and the brown felt tip must have faded and that's why it looks yellow. I should have checked before I showed you."

She leaned forward and gripped Edwin's hand.

"But Edwin, it doesn't matter how you got

to be king, because you're brilliant at it," she said. "You've shown it over and over again. And you'll show it again today."

There was a long silence, broken only by Megan farting in her sleep.

They shook Megan awake, and a minute later, the king, the minister, the jester and the cube were climbing through the icicles, heading for the edge of the platform.

Wendy Worry climbed with them. The imaginary girl, carrying a big cardboard tub of imaginary popcorn.

Oh, it's even better than I thought! said Wendy. *That silly rule that made you king – it's all made up! There's nothing making you king at all – except a **LIE!** You're just a stupid little orphan boy! And you're about to lose everything!*

Edwin peeped over the edge of the platform. There it was, with the ice folk patting the last few bits of snow onto its side – the enormous, colossal, immense, massive, vast, hulking, gargantuan, humongous, really quite large,

Snowball of Doom.

The Snowball of Doom

"Isn't it magnificent?" said Emperor Nurbison. "So huge and white and heavy."

"It'll definitely crush a castle, kind of like, yeah, no bother," said Globulus.

The Snowball of Doom would have been pushed down the mountain about two hours earlier, when Edwin and his friends were only half way to the top, but then the emperor had the fantastic idea to carve his own face into the side of the snowball.

"The last thing Edwin and those peasants will see is my head," said the emperor, "but three hundred metres wide and zooming down from the sky! Soon the only castle in these lands will be mine! Foo Hoo Hoo Hoo!"

Emperor Nurbison leapt out of his frozen lightning throne, surprising the foxes, which dashed around in his boxer shorts and gave Nurbison a terrible itch down below.

"Ice folk, assemble!" said the emperor, trying hard not to scratch his itchy bum while everyone was watching.

The ice folk gathered.

"Nobody's seen Cube all day," said Chief Crystalface. "Emperor, have you seen him?"

"The snowball is complete!" said Nurbison, pretending he hadn't heard the question, a favourite trick of scumbags everywhere. "Now, fetch the long icicle poles! One little poke will get the snowball rolling, then it'll bounce down the mountain all the way to Edwin's castle, and then . . . ker-splat-oom! Or whatever noise a giant snowball makes! We'll find out in a minute, I suppose! Foo hoo hoo hoo!"

King Edwin, Megan, Jill and Cube came
running across the platform.

"Everybody stop!" said Cube.

"I am King Edwin Flashypants," said King
Edwin Flashypants, "and I mean you no harm!"

"GAH! Edwin, what are you doing here?"
said the emperor. "Why don't you have the good
manners to stay in your castle so I can squish
you? Tsk, children today."

"I know what he's been
telling you," said the king
to all the ice folk, "but
it's not true. I don't

drink a mug of lava with my breakfast, or wash my hair in boiling shampoo, and I don't have a spaceship, so I can't take holidays on the surface of the sun."

"Most of all, he's not building a big machine to boil the world," said Megan. "If he was, I'd know about it. Unless he was hiding it in a cupboard, and kings *do* have huge cupboards. You're not hiding a world-boiling machine, are you Edwin? Oh, Jill's giving me a stare like she wants me to stop talking. I'll stop talking. I'll stop straight away. That's what I shall do. Yes."

The ice folk looked from Edwin to Nurbison, from Nurbison to Edwin. Who should they believe?

"Hey, that's, you know, kind of weird," said Globulus to the emperor. "Edwin looks sort of chunky. You know. A bit tubby. And he's making a sort of sloshy sound when he moves. Yeah."

"Aha! I know why," said Nurbison. "Hand me a bolt of lightning, Globulus."

Globulus snapped a zig-zag of frozen lightning off the throne and tossed it to the emperor.

"Why," said Nurbison, "Edwin the Hot is so utterly scorching that even his blood is boiling. Look!"

The emperor slashed Edwin's coat with his lightning spear. Not enough to hurt Edwin – but just deep enough to slice through the hot water bottles keeping the boy warm.

Nurbison pressed his big hand against
Edwin. Jets of scalding water shot out of the
king's coat and made a huge cloud of boiling
steam on the icy platform.

"And the rest of them are the same, look!"
Nurbison danced about, ripping open the

coats of Megan and Jill. Hot water sprayed everywhere, and nobody could see through the big cloud of hot steam that it made.

There was total panic on the mountain top.

Shrieking ice folk ran in circles, bashing Edwin, Megan and Jill this way and that.

Nurbison was knocked over again and again, which bashed the foxes in his coat, who got so frightened they bit the emperor all over.

"As soon as – OW! – the steam blows away, all – OW! – ice folk get ready to push the – OW! – snowball!" said Nurbison.

Edwin couldn't see Megan, or Jill, or Cube. He couldn't even see his hands in front of him. But he could hear Wendy Worry, shouting in his ear through big mouthfuls of imaginary popcorn:

Oh, you'll do anything to stop that snowball, won't you? You'll stand right in front of it if you have to. But you can't see. You're lost, just like in the blizzard. You'll never guess which way is the right way!

EATING WITH MOUTH FULL (VERY BAD)

Edwin ran through the steam, almost fell over the edge of the ice platform, then turned around.

"Emperor Nurbison!" said King Edwin, into the foggy air. "If you want to roll that snowball and crush my castle and everyone in it . . . you'll have to crush me first!"

"Deal!" said the emperor. "Ice folk – we all heard where that voice came from. Push the snowball that way!"

The ice folk heaved with their long ice poles and the colossal snowball began to roll.

"And now it's rolling, nothing can stop it! Foo hoo hoo hoo!" said Emperor Nurbison.

Edwin jumped out of its way.

And at that moment, a gust of wind finally blew the cloud of steam from the top of Hetherang.

Everyone watched the snowball as it bounced down the mountain with a boom, boom, boom. Heading for a castle.

Emperor Nurbison's castle.

"What?" said Nurbison.

What? said Wendy Worry.

"Umm, kind of like, you know, sort of err, what?" said Globulus.

You said it was like in the blizzard, Wendy, thought Edwin. *You said I'd never guess the right way. And I thought: yeah, Wendy's right. I **will** choose the wrong way. So then all I had to do was decide which way my castle is, check I was totally sure I'd chosen the right way . . . then* *that would be totally the wrong way. The way to*

Nurbison's *castle.*

So you used your wrongness to win, said
Wendy. *That's pretty smart. I didn't think of that.*

"Globulus!" screamed the emperor. "Stop that giant handsome snowball with my face on it! It's going to crush **my** castle!"

"Yeah, that is kind of, a bit bad, for sure," said Globulus. "And you know, I'm bummed out about it too cause all my stuff is in there. But didn't you kind of say that once it's rolling, nothing can, you know, stop it?"

"I know what I said," said Emperor

169

Nurbison. "Just do something!"

Nurbison shook all the foxes out of his cloak.

"Foxes! Do something," he said.

The foxes blinked. Then ran away.

"You ice folk! You do something!" said Nurbison.

"Yeah, okay," said Cube.

Cube kind-of-accidentally-but-not-really-accidentally pushed the emperor off the mountain.

"SCRUNGE!" yelled the emperor as he fell. "SCRUNGING CLOFFBODGE! CLOFFBODGING SCRUUUUNNNNNGE!"

And a few seconds later, the whole world shook as the Snowball of Doom landed right on the emperor's castle – with a huge, deafening **KER-SPLAT-OOM**.

11.

What We've All Learned

After Edwin, Jill, Megan and Cube had explained everything to the ice folk, Chief Crystalface stood tapping her chin, which made a pleasant chiming noise.

"King Edwin, we were very wrong about you," said the chief.

"That's okay," said Edwin. "I'm wrong about me half the time, too."

"The ice folk need a chief who judges other people better than I do," she said.

"Ice folk – who will be your new chief?"

The ice folk tinkled at each other for a minute, then spoke with one voice.

"All hail Chief Cube!"

"Umm, hey everyone," said Globulus, "the emperor kind of needs me right now, yeah, and I'm up on this mountain, so can somebody, like, kick me over the edge?"

"You can just climb down if you like, Globulus," said Chief Cube.

"But I'm the exact size and shape of a beach ball," said Globulus. "So, you know, it would be a bit of a waste to *not* kick me."

So Crystalface kicked Globulus over the edge.

"Stay in touch, Cube mate," said Globulus as he fell.

"Totally," said Cube.

"Let's get home and tell everyone they're safe now," said Jill.

Crystalface fetched something very colourful and very curved.

"Here. Emperor Nurbison didn't want to use it."

Edwin definitely did. A minute later, the ice folk waved goodbye as the king, the jester and the minister sledged down the side of Hetherang on a piece of frozen rainbow.

If I was asked to dream up something which meant 'feeling good', thought Edwin, *then sledging down a mountain on a frozen rainbow might be what I came up with. Well, that or a disco on a boat. Or having a splurge gun fight in a hall of mirrors. Okay, I can dream of lots of fun things, but this one is top five, easy.*

After they got back to the castle, the air felt a tiny bit warmer. Warm enough for everyone to finally run out of the castle and make snowmen and snow angels and have a proper old snowball fight. Then everybody gathered in the throne room to hear what Edwin and his friends had learned on their adventures.

Jill stood up first.

"I learned something," she said, "from this letter that's just come from the minister of Rankling La."

Jill read from a long paper scroll.

"Dear Minister Jill, just a note to say that the recent weather was caused by a child who wished for a winter so cold that her bum shattered and fell off. The genie is now under lamp arrest. The child has been told off, and is on the waiting list for a bum transplant. Weather should be back to normal soon."

The emperor's old peasants and soldiers all stood up at once.

"We've learned something," they all said in perfect unison. "We've learnt not to put up with bullies. If you don't like them, walk away and find better friends."

Megan the Jester stood.

"I've learned absolutely loads again, I expect!" said Megan.

Edwin was the last to stand.

"I've learned something big this time," said Edwin. "I learned there's no old rule that makes me king. That law about the birthmark was, well, it was a little bit made up."

Everyone except Jill was very surprised. So many eyebrows shot up so fast that twelve or thirteen flew off people's faces, and got stuck in the ceiling.

"It was made up for a good reason. But it means that I'm not really your true king."

Edwin took off his crown and placed it on the throne.

"The ice folk choose their own leaders. Maybe we should do that, too. Everyone have a bit of a chat, work out who'll be best. And thanks, everyone. Just . . . thanks."

Edwin walked slowly to the back of the throne room and sat down on a little stool.

As the people huddled and talked and waved their arms, Edwin thought: *I wonder who they'll pick? Clever Baxter? Jill, always the wisest? Megan? Or loyal Colin? Okay, maybe not Colin. It's not such a great idea to have an actual horse in charge for too long. He was getting everyone to eat hay and jump over fences by the time we got home. But whoever it is, I'll serve them as well as I can.*

Would Edwin miss being king?

Yes, he would. He closed his eyes and took a moment to remember the good bits.

Then he thought: *that's weird. I feel like I'm floating.*

He opened his eyes and looked around. The crowd was carrying him through the room.

And back to the throne.

"By a unanimous decision . . ." said Minister Jill.

"What does 'unanimous' mean again?" said Edwin.

"It means that everybody agrees. Really, Edwin, we did that in your spelling tests," said Jill.

"I almost remember that," said Edwin.

Jill said, "by unanimous decision – we want our ruler to be – King Edwin Flashypants!"

Megan placed the crown on Edwin's head.

The cheering and clapping almost blew the roof off.

Wendy Worry marched up to Edwin's throne.

Edwin! Why aren't you worried? she said. *That's our thing! That's what we do together!*

Wendy, I don't think I'll be needing you for a while, thought Edwin. *Why don't you take a holiday? A very long one.*

Edwin imagined a wheelie suitcase next to Wendy. Then he imagined she was gone.

And then – pop! – she was.

The emperor sat in what was left of his castle. It was part rubble, and part melting slush, and none of it had a roof. Every chair in the place had been smashed to bits, so Nurbison sat on Globulus instead.

"We should do that thing," said Globulus, "you know, what they do in Edwinland, where they talk about what they learned. That."

"Oh, all right then," said Nurbison.

"What I learned, right," said Globulus, "is that when a three hundred metre wide snowball kind of hits a castle, it really does go ker-splat-oom. That really is the right noise. No question. End of."

"I have learned," said Emperor Nurbison, "that when all my peasants and soldiers ran away to join King Edwin, only one person stayed by my side. You."

Deep inside the emperor, there was a very tiny bit of niceness. It was the same part that liked stickers of bears in dungarees. And that nice bit was trying ever so hard to make the

THE GOOD
BIT INSIDE
NURBISON
(NOT LARGE)

emperor's mouth say: *Thank you, Globulus.*

You're my best mate, you are.

But the mouth said: "And so you SHOULD

stay by my side, after all I've done for you!"

A tiny puff of wind came out of the emperor's ear. That was the nice bit inside him, sighing.

"I've also learned," said Nurbison, "that if my castle is destroyed, it's a chance to rebuild everything even better than before. And I think I have an idea for exactly how."

Just what was the emperor's idea?

We will find out.

In another book.

THIS IS A BLANK PAGE
WHERE YOU CAN DRAW
ANYTHING YOU LIKE
OH WAIT I SPOILED
IT BY WRITING THIS
IN THE MIDDLE OF
THE PAGE SO IT'S
NO USE NOW I'M
VERY SORRY

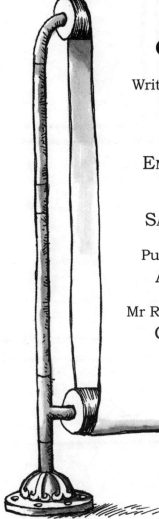

CREDITS

Written and Drawn by
ANDY RILEY

Editor
EMMA GOLDHAWK

Designer
SAMUEL PERRETT

Publishing Director
ANNE MCNEIL

Mr Riley represented by
GORDON WISE

OKAY THIS A BLANK
PAGE WHERE YOU
CAN DRAW ANYTHING
YOU LIKE OH NO
I WROTE IN THE
MIDDLE OF THE
PAGE AGAIN
I AM SUCH AN
IDIOT

ANDY RILEY

ANDY RILEY has done lots of funny writing for film and TV, and he's even won prizes for it, like BAFTAs and an Emmy. He co-wrote the scripts for David Walliams's *Gangsta Granny* and *The Boy In The Dress*. Films he's written for include *Gnomeo & Juliet* and *The Pirates! In An Adventure With Scientists*. He wears cowboy hats a lot, and he's finally going to build a coracle this year, absolutely definitely.

f **www.facebook.com/KingFlashypants**